The Advent Calendar Murder

24 Days, 24 Clues. One Chilling Christmas Mystery

Victor Richard

Table of Contents

Chapter 4 — Silent Nights, Dark Truths

4.1 The Fourth Door Opens

4.2 A Chilling Discovery

4.3 Suspects Multiply

4.4 The Victim's Secret Life

Chapter 5 — Countdown to Panic

5.1 The Town Meeting

5.2 A Break in the Case

5.3 The Calendar Strikes Again

5.4 Betrayal Under the Lights

Chapter 6 — The Final Twelve

6.1 A Race Against Time

6.2 A Clue Hidden in Carol Lyrics

6.3 The Wintervale Archives

6.4 The Killer's Shadow

Chapter 7 — Christmas Eve Confession

Chapter 8 — After the Frost Settles

Chapter 1

The First Door

The Snowfall That Started It All

The first snowfall of December drifted over Pinebrook like a soft white curtain, settling onto rooftops, sidewalks, and the endless rows of pine trees that framed the small town. For most people, it marked the beginning of the holiday season—lights were strung across porches, wreaths hung on doors, and the faint sound of carols drifted from radios and shop windows. Children pressed their noses to frosty glass panes, hoping school might be canceled. Couples drank hot chocolate by firelight. The whole town glowed with tradition and familiarity.

But for **Elena Ward**, the snowfall felt different this year.

She stood at her living-room window, arms wrapped around herself, watching the heavy flakes swirl beneath the pale morning sun. She had always loved winter—the cold air, the quiet blanketing of the world—but now she felt a strange tightness in her chest. A sense that the season was beginning not with joy, but with a shift. A change. Something she couldn't name.

Her black hair fell over her shoulders in loose waves, still messy from sleep. She hadn't bothered to change out of the oversized sweater she'd pulled on the night before. She looked tired—older than thirty-two, though she blamed that on a mixture of overwork and the lingering aftershocks of a life gone slightly off-course.

The snowfall reminded her of her parents' house, of childhood mornings running downstairs to the smell of cinnamon and pine, her mother humming softly as she lit the Advent wreath. An ache flickered beneath her ribs. This was her first December without either of them.

She blinked hard and stepped away from the window.

Her phone buzzed on the countertop. It was a text from her brother, Ethan.

"Call you later. Flight delayed again. Chicago is chaos."

She typed back quickly.

"Stay safe. Let me know when you land."

He was supposed to arrive by the second week of December. They hadn't spent Christmas together in years—not since their mother's health began to decline. Now that both parents were gone, it felt like they were trying to glue together the pieces of something that had fractured long before they realized it.

Elena exhaled slowly and walked toward the kitchen. She turned on the kettle and leaned against the counter, rubbing her hands together for warmth. Outside, the snowfall thickened, casting the town in muted silence.

The kettle whistled. She poured herself a cup of tea and walked back to the window. For a moment, everything looked peaceful.

Then she saw it.

A figure, dressed in a dark coat, crossing her front yard.

Not walking casually. Not delivering a package like the postal workers who usually came in brightly colored winter gear.

This person moved deliberately, the hood pulled low, their face obscured. They walked straight toward her porch—closer, closer—then paused.

They looked up.

Directly at her window.

Elena's breath froze.

The figure didn't wave, didn't nod. They simply *stood there*, head angled toward her, as if examining the outline of her body behind the glass.

Then, just as quickly, they turned and hurried off—leaving something sitting on the porch steps.

A small package.

Wrapped not in holiday paper, but plain brown kraft paper tied with a deep red string.

Her stomach tightened.

It wasn't the mail service. No delivery truck idled nearby. No footsteps echoed from the street.

It was just the snowfall.
And the package.

And the stranger disappearing down the sidewalk.

Elena set her tea aside and grabbed her coat.

Something was wrong.

Very wrong.

A Package on the Porch

The cold hit her like a wall the moment she stepped outside. The air was sharp, stinging her cheeks and filling her lungs with icy clarity. She tugged her coat tighter and scanned the street.

Empty.

The stranger was nowhere in sight.

Her porch creaked beneath her boots as she approached the package with cautious steps. Snowflakes clung to the brown paper, already dampening the corners. The handwriting on the tag was bold and elegant—almost old-fashioned.

To: Elena Ward

That was it.

No return address. No stamp. Nothing to indicate who had delivered it.

Her first impulse was to leave it exactly where it was. But curiosity—or something deeper—nudged her forward. She reached down slowly and lifted it from the step. It was heavier than it looked, about the weight of a thick book.

She felt a shiver crawl down her spine.

Inside the house again, she locked the door behind her and set the package on the dining table. Her fingers hovered over the red string.

"Okay," she whispered to herself, "just open it."

She tugged the string loose.

The paper fell away.

Inside was a beautifully crafted **wooden Advent calendar**—the kind made with tiny doors, intricately carved numbers, and small brass knobs. It looked old, polished, expensive. The wood was dark cherry, and the craftsmanship was exquisite, almost museum quality.

But something about it felt... off.

She ran her fingers over the first small door—marked *1* in gold paint. A faint chill passed through her fingertips, as if the wood itself held onto the cold longer than it should.

Then she noticed the note.

A folded slip of parchment tucked beneath the calendar.

Her name was written on the outside in the same elegant handwriting.

She unfolded it carefully.

**"December begins with truth.
Open Door 1.
Follow every clue.
You cannot run from the past forever."**

Elena stared at the words, her heart pounding. A thousand questions surged through her mind.

Who sent this?

Why did they know her address?

Why did it sound like a threat?

She considered calling Ethan, but he was stuck in an airport hundreds of miles away. She considered calling her best friend, Maisie—but Maisie had toddlers and too much to worry about without adding mysterious packages to the list.

Another thought crossed her mind.
The police.

But what would she say?

"Someone left me a fancy Advent calendar"?
The officer would raise an eyebrow and ask if it was a Secret Santa gift.

No. She needed something more concrete before she dragged anyone into this. A clearer sense of what the calendar *wanted* from her.

Her gaze drifted back to the note.

Open Door 1.

A long moment passed.

Then she reached for the brass knob and pulled.

The tiny door swung open.

Inside, instead of the expected chocolate or trinket, sat a small rolled-up strip of paper. She removed it carefully and smoothed it onto the table.

The writing was the same—sharp, elegant, deliberate.

"Clue One:
 At the heart of every secret is a name.
 Start where your memory falters.
 Someone remembers what you've forgotten."

Elena's pulse hammered in her ears.

Someone was playing a game with her.
 Someone who knew more about her than they should.

But what did they mean about her memories?

She closed the tiny door and stared at the calendar, dread pooling in her stomach like icy water.

This wasn't a gift.

This was a message.

And it wasn't just for fun.

The First Clue

Elena paced the living room, the clue held tightly in her hand.

"At the heart of every secret is a name.
Start where your memory falters.
Someone remembers what you've forgotten."

She repeated the lines aloud. The words curled through the air like smoke.

Her memory faltered?

What memory?

She had lived in Pinebrook her whole life except for three years in college. She knew every street, every face, every tradition. Nothing felt missing, nothing felt forgotten—except the dull edges of grief she was still navigating.

But the clue didn't feel like it was about her parents.
It felt personal—but in a different way.
Older.
Buried.

She pulled out a notebook and wrote the clue down again, underlining the word "name."

Names carried weight.
Names revealed things.

She thought about the Advent calendar again—the craftsmanship, the aged wood, the brass knobs. It looked antique. Valuable. Not something someone would buy off a shelf. Its presence suggested intention. Someone had chosen it specifically for her.

But why?

She grabbed her coat again and stepped outside, scanning the porch for footprints. Snow had piled up quickly, but she could still make out faint impressions leading away from her house and disappearing into the direction of Cedar Street.

The figure had walked with purpose.
No sign of hesitation.

Back inside, she sat at the dining table with the calendar in front of her. She looked again at Door 1. The brass knob was cold beneath her touch.

The clue bothered her more than she wanted to admit. Something about it tugged at a part of her mind she usually avoided. A part she had sealed away long ago.

Her childhood.

The day everything changed.

She swallowed hard.

At age ten, she had witnessed something—something she had tried to forget, something her parents never talked about. A shadowy memory of being at the town's winter carnival, of wandering away from the crowd, of seeing—

No.
Her hands clenched into fists.
She had promised herself she wouldn't go back to that memory.

But what if the clue was pointing her there?

She sighed shakily and opened the calendar again, gently touching the wood around Door 1. She hadn't noticed it earlier, but carved faintly into the frame—so faint it was almost invisible—was a symbol. A tiny engraved snowflake with eight points.

Her breath caught.

She knew that symbol.

Every child in Pinebrook knew it.

The **Pinebrook Winter Festival** used it for their logo.

A festival where the town gathered every year.
 A festival with games, music, rides—
 And one tragedy everyone pretended never happened.

She set the calendar down, her hands trembling.

Someone remembers what you've forgotten.

A name.

Which name?

A knock on the door made her jump.

Her heart slammed into her ribs as she froze, staring at
the doorway.

Another knock.
 Harder this time.

"Elena?" a familiar voice called. "It's Sheriff Dalton."

Relief washed through her, but it was tinged with unease. Why was the sheriff here?

She opened the door. Sheriff Rob Dalton stood there, snow dusting his tan uniform and the brim of his hat. He looked serious—more serious than she'd seen him in years.

"Everything okay?" Elena asked.

Dalton nodded once, but his eyes flicked behind her into the house. "We got a report about a suspicious person walking through the neighborhood earlier. Dark coat, hood up, moving between yards."

Her blood ran cold.

She stepped back, letting him inside.

"I saw someone," she whispered. "They left... something."

Dalton raised an eyebrow. "Something?"

She gestured toward the dining table. The sheriff walked over and examined the Advent calendar without touching it. His face didn't change, but his jaw tightened a fraction.

"Who delivered this?" he asked.

Elena shook her head. "I have no idea. They just appeared in my yard and left it."

"And you didn't recognize them?"

"No."

"Did they see you?"

She hesitated. "Yes. They looked right at me."

Dalton exhaled slowly. "That's not good."

She swallowed. "Do you think it's dangerous?"

"Could be nothing," he said, though his tone didn't match his words. "Or it could be someone playing a very strange game."

He leaned closer to the calendar. "Mind if I take a look?"

"Go ahead."

Dalton opened Door 1 and read the clue silently. His expression darkened.

"You said someone left this for *you*?" he asked.

"Yes."

"And you didn't tell anyone you were expecting anything?"

"No," she repeated. "Why?"

Dalton folded the paper again and slipped it back inside the tiny compartment.

"Because," he said quietly, "this handwriting looks familiar."

Elena stared at him, confused. "Familiar how?"

Dalton hesitated for a long moment.

Then he said the name she had tried so hard to forget.

"Thomas Weller."

Her breath hitched.

No.
Impossible.
Thomas Weller had died twenty-two years ago.

At the Winter Festival.

The same year Elena's memory fractured.

She grabbed the edge of the table. "That's not possible."

Dalton shook his head. "I know. But his case files... this handwriting is almost identical."

Elena felt the room tilt.

The past she had buried was clawing its way back up, one clue at a time.

A Town on Edge

Sheriff Dalton stayed for nearly an hour, asking questions, jotting down notes, and studying the Advent calendar with increasing concern. Elena answered everything as best she could, though her mind buzzed with confusion and fear.

Thomas Weller.

The name alone made her stomach twist.

He had been seventeen. A quiet boy. Kept to himself. Some people said he was odd, but kind. Others said he knew things—noticed things. He had been found dead at the Winter Festival, the same night Elena had wandered off, the same night her memory hit a blank wall she'd never been able to climb over.

The case had never been officially solved.

Dalton was only a rookie then, but he remembered the handwriting in Weller's journals and notebooks—spirals of elegant letters, loops, flourishes. And now an Advent calendar, delivered mysteriously to Elena, used that same script.

When Dalton finally left, promising to patrol the area and "keep an eye on things," Elena locked the door again and sank onto the sofa.

Her house felt too quiet.
 Too still.

She grabbed a blanket and wrapped it around herself, staring at the Advent calendar still sitting on the dining table.

Outside, the snowfall had turned into a heavy storm. The wind howled softly, rattling the windows. Pinebrook, usually cheerful this time of year, felt uneasy. As if the town sensed a disturbance in the fabric of its traditions.

She wasn't the only one who felt it. She had seen the way Dalton had scanned the street before leaving, how his hand hovered near his holster. Something had unsettled him—and Dalton didn't unsettle easily.

Elena closed her eyes.

A memory stirred.
Faint.
Through the fog of childhood fear.

A carnival ride.
Bright lights.
Her small hand gripping a paper bag of caramel popcorn.
A shadow moving behind the trees.
A voice whispering her name.

She flinched.

Was the Advent calendar connected to that night?

She walked to the window and peered outside. Only snow greeted her. The stranger was gone. The world looked innocent again, but she no longer believed the illusion.

The calendar sat on the table like a living thing.

Door 1 was open.
Twenty-three more doors remained.

Twenty-three clues.
Twenty-three days until Christmas.

If the first clue had shaken her this deeply, what would
the others reveal?

She returned to the dining table, her fingers brushing
against the polished wood.

The town was on edge.
The sheriff was uneasy.
Old names were resurfacing.
Old secrets were waking.

A storm had arrived—
and it wasn't just outside.

Elena inhaled shakily and whispered to herself:

"I need to know the truth."

Even if the truth was buried beneath decades of snow.

Even if it was tied to a name that should've stayed dead.

Even if it meant facing the past she had spent twenty-two years trying to forget.

The Advent calendar awaited her.

And someone out there—someone watching—wanted her to open every door.

The first one had been unsettling.

The next twenty-three would be worse.

Elena sat down, picked up the clue again, and stared at the elegant handwriting:

Someone remembers what you've forgotten.

Her voice trembled as she whispered:

"Who are you?"

But the calendar, like the town, remained silent.

For now.

Chapter 2

Secrets Beneath the Tinsel

The Detective Arrives

Morning came slow and gray, the kind of winter morning that felt thick and heavy, as if the sun had to push through layers of cloud to breathe. Elena had barely slept—her mind kept circling the Advent calendar like a moth around a flame. Every time she closed her eyes, she saw the elegant handwriting, the stranger in the snow, the sheriff's uneasy expression.

Her tea had gone cold on the nightstand. She tossed the blankets aside and stepped into her slippers, rubbing her face with tired hands. She felt wrung out, like someone had pressed her against a wall and held her there all night.

By the time she made it downstairs, it was nearly ten. The house felt too quiet again. The Advent calendar still sat on the dining table, its polished wood gleaming in the pale light. She avoided looking directly at it as she walked into the kitchen.

The kettle had just begun to hum when she heard a car pull into her driveway.

Her stomach clenched.

She walked quickly to the window.

A dark sedan. Unmarked.

A tall figure stepped out—broad-shouldered, wearing a charcoal-gray coat dusted with snowflakes. His hair was dark and neatly cut, his posture firm and deliberate. He scanned her house once, then started toward the front door.

A knock followed—three measured beats.

Elena hesitated before opening it.

"Ms. Ward?" the man asked, his voice calm and steady.

"Yes?"

He showed her a badge. "Detective Asher Cole. Pinebrook Police Department. Sheriff Dalton asked me to stop by. May I come in?"

Relief and uncertainty tangled inside her.

"Yes... of course."

Detective Cole stepped inside, closing the door gently behind him. He was tall—well over six feet—with sharp features softened only slightly by the warmth in his brown eyes. Snowflakes melted on his coat as he glanced around her entryway with quiet observation.

"Dalton told you to come?" she asked, folding her arms.

"Sheriff Dalton said you received an unusual delivery yesterday. He asked me to look into it."

Elena nodded slowly.

Cole added, "Dalton's tied up downtown right now. Busy morning. But he wanted someone experienced to come assess the situation."

"You're... experienced?" she asked before she could stop herself.

A corner of his mouth lifted. "I've been with the department twelve years. Before that, I worked in Boston for eight. Strange cases are my specialty."

Strange.

That felt like an understatement.

Elena motioned him inside. "It's on the dining table."

Cole walked ahead, his boots quiet on the hardwood floor. He stopped in front of the Advent calendar, studying it with a stillness that made Elena uneasy. He didn't touch it—not yet.

"This is beautiful craftsmanship," he murmured. "Definitely handmade. Looks old—late nineteenth or early twentieth century."

Elena felt a chill. "How can you tell?"

"The wood, the joinery, the style of numbering. And the brass knobs—they're not modern." He leaned closer. "Where did this come from?"

"That's the problem," she said. "I don't know."

Cole nodded. "Dalton said someone in a hooded coat delivered it?"

"Yes," she said. "They walked right into my yard. Looked at me. Then left."

"And left... this." Cole tapped the table lightly beside it, careful not to touch the calendar itself.

"Yes."

He finally crouched, examining the tiny carved snowflake symbol near Door 1. "This symbol looks familiar," he said.

Elena swallowed. "It's from the Pinebrook Winter Festival logo."

He stood slowly, a faint crease forming between his eyebrows. "You noticed that too?"

"Is that important?"

Cole didn't answer directly. Instead, he asked, "Did you open any doors?"

"Just the first one."

"And inside?"

"A note."

"May I see it?"

Elena nodded and retrieved the small rolled strip of paper from where she'd tucked it into her notebook. She handed it to him.

Cole unrolled it, his eyes scanning each word carefully.

His jaw tightened. "This is no prank."

"That's what Dalton said," Elena whispered.

Cole rolled the paper back up and set it gently on the table. Then he looked at her, his expression turning serious in a way that made her breath catch.

"Elena," he said, his tone softer but resolute, "this message was written by someone with intent. Someone who knows you. Someone who wants you involved."

"Involved in what?" she asked. "Some kind of game?"

"Games don't usually come wrapped in threats."

Elena's stomach dropped. "You think it's a threat?"

Cole didn't sugarcoat. "I think someone is trying to push you toward something. Or push something toward you."

She felt a tremor run through her arms.

He took a step closer. "I need you to tell me everything you can remember about yesterday. Every detail about the person who delivered this. And anything about your past that could be connected."

She swallowed. "My past?"

"Yes."

Her heartbeat quickened.

There *was* something.
Something she hadn't told Dalton.
Something she rarely let herself think about.

Cole waited.

Elena exhaled shakily. "Do you know the name Thomas Weller?"

Cole's expression shifted—recognition flickering like a flame.

"Yes," he said quietly. "I know the name."

Elena nodded, her voice barely above a whisper. "Dalton thinks the handwriting might match his."

Cole's eyes hardened. "That case should've stayed buried."

"What do you mean?"

Cole didn't answer immediately. He walked slowly around the table, his hands in his coat pockets, his gaze distant.

"Because," he finally said, "Thomas Weller's death was ruled accidental. But many people—myself included—never believed that."

Elena felt her chest tighten.

"And now," Cole continued softly, "it seems his story isn't finished."

Whispered Rumors in Wintervale

Detective Cole insisted on accompanying her to town. "If someone is watching you," he said, "it's better if they see you're not alone." The way he said it made Elena's skin prickle.

Pinebrook's downtown—called *Wintervale* during the holiday season—was already decorated with strings of white lights, red bows, garlands, and a towering Christmas tree in the center square. Normally, she loved this time of year: the bustling shops, the smell of roasted chestnuts, children laughing as they hurried between decorated stalls.

But today, everything felt... off.

Too cheerful. Too bright.
Like the decorations were a sugary frosting hiding something rotten underneath.

Cole walked beside her, calm and quiet, but she sensed tension in the way his eyes scanned the crowd.

"You think they're here?" Elena whispered.

"I think whoever delivered that calendar is keeping an eye on you," Cole said. "People don't orchestrate something that deliberate and walk away."

His tone made her tense.

They passed Snowberry Café, the bakery where Elena sometimes worked remote while sipping chai. The owner, Mrs. Flora Helms, waved them inside.

"Elena! Dear, you look pale as the snow outside!" Flora exclaimed, bustling around the counter with her usual grandmotherly energy. Her blue apron was dusted with flour, her cheeks rosy from the oven's heat. "Come sit, come sit. Let me get you something warm."

Elena forced a small smile and took a seat by the window. Cole sat across from her, angled where he could see the doorway.

Flora set two steaming mugs in front of them. "Peppermint mocha for you," she said to Elena, "and black coffee for the gentleman. Now—tell me why the sheriff is roaming around early and why you've brought a detective with you."

Elena hesitated.

Cole gave her a subtle nod—permission to share only what she felt safe sharing.

"A strange package was left at my door yesterday," she said carefully. "Sheriff Dalton wasn't sure what to make of it. Detective Cole is helping."

Flora's bright expression dimmed. "A package?"

"Yes."

"From who?"

"We don't know."

Flora crossed her arms, suddenly serious. "This town's been too quiet lately. December makes people restless." Her eyes darted toward a small group of older women whispering near the pastry case. "Rumors start up as soon as the lights go on."

"What kind of rumors?" Cole asked, leaning slightly forward.

Flora lowered her voice. "The kind that make people talk about old tragedies." She wiped her hands on her apron. "Some folks say that this winter feels... familiar."

Elena's breath caught. "Familiar how?"

Flora gave her a long look. "Like twenty-two years ago."

Cole straightened. "You mean Thomas Weller."

The name made the whispering group at the counter go silent for a moment, then resume even more quietly.

Flora's expression tightened. "Don't say it too loudly."

"Why?" Elena asked.

Flora leaned in. "Because some people think his spirit never left."

Elena stared. "You mean like a ghost?"

Flora gave her a thin smile. "Every town has its stories. Some folks say they've seen him in the snow over the years. A boy with a hood pulled up, walking between houses, watching."

Cole's jaw tightened. "Superstition. Nothing more."

"Maybe." Flora shrugged. "But Pinebrook has always been a place where memories linger. And some memories don't like staying buried."

Elena swallowed hard.

Flora changed the subject quickly, as if worried she'd said too much. "You two eat something. You look like you need it."

But Elena couldn't eat.
 Her mocha sat untouched.
 Her mind buzzed with Flora's words.

Some memories don't like staying buried.

Detective Cole took a sip of his coffee, his eyes drifting out the window toward the swirling snow. "People see what they want to see," he said quietly. "Rumors fill the gaps. But I don't chase ghosts."

"What do you chase?" Elena asked softly.

He met her eyes.

"Truth."

She nodded, feeling something inside her steady—just a little. Cole wasn't dismissive, nor was he gullible. He existed in the space between logic and intuition, and somehow, that made her trust him.

When they left the café, a few locals watched them go, their expressions a blend of concern and curiosity. Pinebrook loved gossip, but this flavor of gossip—the kind wrapped in fear—felt heavier.

As they walked toward the town square, Elena felt the chill deepening. Not just from the air, but from the sense that eyes watched her from the corners of windows, from behind curtains, from doorways.

Not human eyes.
 Not exactly.

Eyes of memory.

Of something Pinebrook had never truly forgotten.

Detective Cole noticed her shiver. "You okay?"

"No," she admitted quietly. "It feels like the whole town is holding its breath."

Cole didn't disagree.

He just said, "That's because it is."

The Calendar's Hidden Message

Back at her house, the Advent calendar felt colder than before. As if the wood itself had chilled during their absence.

Cole removed his gloves and crouched beside the table again. "I want to check for hidden compartments."

Elena's eyes widened. "Hidden compartments?"

"These older calendars sometimes have them," he said. "Especially handcrafted ones. And given the nature of the clue... someone might have left more than what's behind the daily doors."

He examined the sides carefully, running his fingertips along the edges, tapping lightly to listen for hollow spaces.

Elena paced behind him, her nerves taut.

"Cole..." she whispered. "What if we're wrong? What if this is all... coincidence?"

Cole didn't look up. "I don't believe in coincidences this precise."

He tapped near the base—once, twice—and froze.

A different sound.

Hollow.

Elena's breath caught.

Cole slid his fingers beneath the wooden base and found a seam, nearly invisible to the eye. With a gentle push, the panel shifted open.

A hidden compartment.

Inside was a folded piece of paper, thicker than normal parchment, tied with a red thread.

Cole removed it with care. He untied the thread and unfolded the page on the table.

The handwriting was the same elegant style.

"Truth sleeps beneath the snow.
But not forever.
Door 2 holds what Door 1 began.
Look deeper—
for the second clue is not where you expect."

Elena felt her knees weaken. She gripped the back of a chair.

Cole studied the note intensely. "This was meant to be found after you opened the first door."

"What does it mean?" she whispered.

"'Not where you expect' suggests Door 2 won't have the next clue."

"Then where will it be?" Elena asked, her voice wavering.

Cole lifted the calendar, examined the underside again, then glanced toward the room.

"Elena," he said slowly, "has anything in your house been moved? Anything out of place?"

She hesitated.

Then nodded.

"Yes."

Cole stood. "Show me."

She led him to the living room. "Yesterday morning, before the package arrived... I noticed the bookshelf looked different. Like someone shifted things around."

Cole scanned the shelves, his eyes sharp. "Which items?"

"That book there." She pointed. "It used to be on the bottom shelf. And that candle holder—I don't remember putting it in the middle."

Cole walked closer. "May I?"

"Go ahead."

He began inspecting each shelf methodically. Elena watched anxiously as he examined the items one by one.

Then he stopped.

Behind an old copy of *A Christmas Carol*—a book she hadn't opened in years—was something thin sticking out just barely from behind the spine.

A slip of paper.

Cole retrieved it carefully.

Another clue.

He handed it to Elena silently.

Her fingers trembled as she unfolded it.

"Clue Two:
You saw something long ago.
Something the snow tried to hide.
Return to where the memory froze.
The night the lights went out."

Elena's mouth went dry.

"The lights..." she whispered.

Cole met her gaze. "What happened the night the lights went out?"

Elena swallowed hard. "The Winter Festival. Twenty-two years ago."

"The same night Thomas Weller died," Cole said.

Elena nodded slowly, fear creeping into her chest like frost.

"That night," she whispered, "I got lost behind the carnival tents. And... someone turned off the lights."

She pressed a hand to her forehead. "I heard something. Or someone."

Cole stepped closer, his voice low but steady. "What did you hear?"

She shut her eyes tight.

A whisper.
Her name.
A shadow moving.
Her ten-year-old heart pounding.

"I don't know," she whispered. "I was too scared. I ran."

"And Thomas Weller?" Cole asked.

Elena's voice cracked. "I never saw him. But they said he was last seen near the trees. Near where I was."

Cole inhaled slowly, his expression darkening. "Elena... someone believes you know more than you think. Someone wants you to remember."

"I don't want to remember," she admitted, tears threatening.

"But you might have to," Cole said gently. "Because whoever sent this believes you saw something that night. Something important."

Elena wiped her eyes with the back of her hand. "Why now? After all these years?"

Cole looked at the calendar.

"At Christmas, secrets are harder to keep," he said softly. "And some ghosts finally find their voice."

A Past No One Mentions

Elena sat on the couch, knees pulled to her chest, the second clue lying on the coffee table. The words seemed to pulse in the dim light.

Return to where the memory froze.

Detective Cole paced in front of the fireplace, deep in thought.

"You were ten," he said. "Children remember more than adults give them credit for. But trauma buries details. Sometimes deliberately."

Elena nodded. "I've tried for years to recall what happened. But I can't. It's like hitting a locked door."

"And now someone is trying to unlock it."

She shivered.

Cole sat across from her. "Tell me everything you remember from that night."

Elena inhaled shakily.

"I remember the lights," she began. "The giant string of bulbs hanging across the trees. They were bright—so bright they made everything look like gold."

Cole nodded. "Go on."

"And the rides. The music. The smell of caramel." Her voice softened. "My mom was holding my hand. My dad was taking pictures. Ethan was eating cotton candy."

She closed her eyes.

"Then someone bumped into me. Hard. I let go of my mom's hand. And suddenly the crowd swallowed me."

Cole leaned forward. "Do you remember who bumped into you?"

"No. Just... a coat. Dark. Maybe navy."

"And then?"

"I wandered toward the trees. I thought my parents would see me better there. But it was darker. Quieter."

Cole waited patiently.

"Then the lights flickered," she whispered. "All at once. And then they went out."

The memory hit her like a cold wave—blurry at first, then sharper.

"I heard footsteps," she said. "Behind me. Crunching in the snow. Slow."

Her voice trembled.

"I turned. And... I think I saw someone. But it was dark. Just a shape. A shadow."

Cole's eyes sharpened. "A man or a boy?"

"I don't know," she said helplessly. "But I remember the feeling. Cold. Like everything inside me froze."

"And then?" he prompted gently.

"I ran," she whispered. "I ran until I saw the carnival lights come back on. And then I found my parents. I didn't tell them anything. I just cried."

Cole sat back slowly, his jaw tight.

"That was the same time Thomas Weller went missing," he said. "He wasn't found until after midnight."

Elena shivered violently. "Do you think I saw him? Or the person who—"

She couldn't finish.

Cole answered carefully. "I think it's possible the shadow you saw was connected. But you were a child. No one expected you to understand."

Elena looked up, tears welling. "Then why send me clues now? Why drag me into this?"

Cole hesitated.

Then said, "Because someone believes you're the key. Someone who was there. Someone who remembers more than you do."

Her blood ran cold.

"But who?" she whispered.

A knock at the door startled them both.

Not gentle.
 Not polite.

Three sharp bangs.

Cole rose instantly, hand near his holster. "Stay here."

Elena watched from the living room as he approached the door carefully, peering through the small window beside it.

After a moment, he opened it a crack.

Sheriff Dalton entered, snow covering his shoulders, his expression severe.

"Cole. Elena."

Elena stood quickly. "Sheriff? What happened?"

Dalton removed his hat, his eyes dark. "We have a situation."

Cole's posture tensed. "What kind of situation?"

Dalton exhaled heavily.

"A body was found."

Elena's stomach twisted.

"Where?" Cole asked sharply.

Dalton hesitated before answering.

"At the edge of the pinewoods. Near the old festival grounds."

Elena felt the world tilt.

Dalton's gaze softened as he turned to her. "Elena... the victim was holding something."

Her breath caught. "What?"

Dalton looked between them.

"A small wooden door," he said quietly. "With the number 2 carved into it."

Elena's knees nearly gave out.

"From *your* calendar," Dalton added.

Cole stepped closer to her instantly. "It's escalating."

Dalton nodded grimly. "This isn't just about the past anymore."

Elena stared at them, fear swelling like a storm inside her.

Someone had taken Door 2 from her Advent calendar.

Someone had left it in a dead man's hand.

A message.

A warning.

Or both.

The room felt colder.
 The shadows deeper.
 The air heavier.

Detective Cole placed a steady hand on her shoulder.

"Elena," he said quietly, "we're running out of time."

And as the snow fell harder outside, blanketing
Pinebrook in white, Elena realized something with
chilling certainty—

December had only just begun.

Chapter 3

The Third Day Revelation

A Coded Warning

Wintervale woke on the third day of December to a sky the color of pewter and a silence so deep it felt intentional. The kind of silence that didn't merely accompany snowfall, but *watched* it. Streets lay blanketed in perfect white, completely unbroken except for the faintest trail of footprints leading from the churchyard to the town square—footprints too small to belong to Detective Hale, too uneven to be a child's playful steps.

By now, everyone in Wintervale knew about the calendar.

They knew about the mysterious package left on Clara Linden's porch.
They knew it contained something more than harmless riddles.
And they knew—whether they admitted it or

not—that Wintervale's calm Christmas season had
been ruptured.

What they didn't know was that each clue seemed
designed for someone.
Someone specific.
Someone the sender believed owed them something.

Detective Elias Hale stood outside the Inn at
Wintervale, the advent calendar box tucked beneath his
arm, cold air stinging his face. The doors were still
locked, the inn not yet open for breakfast. He hadn't
slept more than two hours. Too much didn't add up.

The calendar itself was handcrafted—intricate,
wooden, with tiny brass hinges and a design carved
with remarkable precision. Each door contained a slip
of parchment with cryptic writing executed in the same
exact hand. The wood smelled faintly of pine and
varnish, but also of something faintly metallic.
Something old.

Door Three—opened at 6:04 a.m.—held something
different.

Not a clue.
 Not a symbol.
 But a warning.

A thin strip of parchment held just four words:

"DON'T TRUST THE CHEERFUL."

Nothing else. No signature. No riddle. No playful
rhyme like the previous two.

Hale folded the parchment and tucked it back into the
envelope as two children ran past, throwing handfuls
of snow at each other. Their laughter echoed through
the square, innocent and sharp. It made the warning
feel even more sinister.

"Detective!"

Clara Linden's voice cut through the still air.

She approached, bundled in a thick maroon coat,
cheeks flushed from the cold. Her light brown hair was
pulled into a tight braid and dusted with snowflakes
that hadn't yet melted.

"You saw today's clue?" she asked breathlessly.

"If you can call it a clue," Hale replied, handing it to her.

Clara read it, blinking twice. "Don't trust the cheerful? What is that supposed to mean?"

"I was hoping you'd tell me."

She shook her head. "I have no idea. But... it feels different. Like whoever wrote the other clues was enjoying the mystery. This one feels like a threat."

"Or a warning," Hale said. "But not necessarily to you."

Clara frowned. "Then who?"

"That," he said, "is what we're going to figure out."

He watched her shoulders tense as she handed the parchment back. Clara was a schoolteacher—sharp, warm, dependable—and yet there was a quiet heaviness in her eyes. Something like buried worry. She had received the calendar, yes, but Hale was increasingly certain that the sender's intentions weren't about her specifically.

"Did you notice the footprints in the snow?" Hale asked.

"Near the churchyard? Yes... but they don't go far. Fresh, though. Made after sunrise."

Hale nodded. "That means someone was out early. Too early for casual walking."

Clara's brow furrowed. "Do you think they're from whoever delivered door three's message?"

"Maybe," he said. "Or maybe someone watching us."

The wind swept through the square, and Clara hugged her coat tighter.

"Detective Hale... do you really think we're in danger?"

Hale didn't want to scare her—but sugarcoating wasn't an option anymore.

"I think Wintervale is becoming the stage for something someone planned a long time ago."

"And the advent calendar is just the beginning?"

He met her gaze. "Yes."

Her breath hitched.

Because deep down, Clara had already sensed that truth.

And now, she wasn't alone in fearing it.

An Unexpected Ally

The Wintervale Police Department didn't expect company that morning, especially not a tall woman with a leather satchel, a fast stride, and an expression that looked like it had no time for hesitation.

The desk sergeant looked up. "Can I help you?"

"I'm looking for Detective Hale."

"Name?"

"Dr. Mara Keats."

The sergeant blinked. "As in... *that* Mara Keats? Criminal psychology?"

"Yes," she snapped, "and I'd prefer not to be recognized today. Is the detective here or not?"

Hale stepped into the lobby at the perfect moment.

"Mara?" he said, almost surprised.

She turned, her sharp green eyes softening just slightly. "Elias."

They had worked together once—years ago—on a case involving coded messages and a serial threat. She had been the profiler who cracked the sender's psychological patterns. She had also been the person Hale might have ended up with, if the job hadn't gotten in the way.

"What are you doing here?" Hale asked.

"I heard Wintervale was having... a situation." Her gaze drifted to the advent calendar under his arm. "And when I saw the photo of door two in the regional bulletin, I knew I recognized the pattern."

"You recognized the writing?" Hale asked, stunned.

She shook her head. "No. I recognized the method."

She pulled out a small notebook and opened it to a page covered with symbols almost identical to the carvings on the calendar doors.

"What is this?" Hale asked.

"A case I worked on ten years ago," Mara said. "A case that was never solved."

The sergeant cleared his throat. "Detective, you two can use Conference Room B."

Inside the room, Mara closed the blinds before sitting down. It was a habit of hers—privacy first. Always.

She tapped the carved symbols drawn in her notebook. "Your advent calendar isn't just a holiday craft. It's using a cipher system created by a man named Rowan Vexley."

"Never heard of him," Hale said.

"You wouldn't have," Mara replied. "He was a seasonal artisan who made custom wooden calendars, puzzle boxes, and coded games during the early 2000s. Small-time. Niche. But brilliant. And one of his clients ended up dead."

Hale stiffened. "You think he's connected to this?"

"I think someone is recreating his work," she said. "And whoever it is... they want attention."

Clara, who had been invited to sit in, spoke softly. "Attention from who?"

Mara's gaze landed on her like a scalpel. "From someone with a past they haven't confronted."

Hale thumbed the parchment from door three. "And what do you make of today's message?"

Mara read it twice.

Then her expression changed.

"This isn't a threat," she whispered. "It's a warning. And it's not for you, Detective."

She turned to Clara.

"It's for someone in Wintervale who pretends to be friendly. Someone whose cheerfulness is a disguise."

Clara swallowed hard. "You mean... one of us?"

Mara nodded. "Yes. And the sender wants that person to know they're being watched."

Clara felt a shiver run up her spine, but not from the cold.

Someone in Wintervale was hiding something.

And someone else knew exactly what it was.

Patterns in the Clues

Hale spread the first three clues on the table:

- **Door One:** A blood-red snowflake symbol

- **Door Two:** A riddle referencing a secret kept "under winter's breath"

- **Door Three:** *Don't trust the cheerful.*

Mara studied them with the intensity of someone parsing the mind of a criminal she already hated.

"This sender is clever," she said. "But also emotional. Every choice—every symbol—has meaning."

"What about the snowflake?" Clara asked.

"The snowflake isn't just decoration," Mara replied. "Look closely."

She passed Hale a magnifying glass.

The snowflake had eight arms, each with a miniature notch carved into it.

Hale counted them. "Eight notches... eight victims?"

Mara shook her head. "Eight *years*."

Hale's eyes widened. "You're saying the sender has been planning this for eight years?"

"Or holding onto something that long," she said. "Grief. Rage. Betrayal. Something powerful enough to shape their entire identity."

She slid the snowflake drawing next to the second clue.

"The second clue shows secrecy. Covered tracks. Hidden truths."

Then she pointed to the third.

"And the third? It names the trigger. The person the sender despises the most."

Clara looked between them nervously. "But Wintervale is a small town. People here know each other. *Really* know each other."

Mara leaned back. "People rarely know each other as well as they think."

Her words hung in the room like frost.

Hale paced slowly, processing. "So we're looking for someone cheerful. Outgoing. Someone who uses friendliness like armor."

Clara bit her lower lip.

"What?" Hale asked.

"There's someone like that," she admitted. "Someone who's... overly cheerful. Forced, almost. But if I say it out loud, it might sound unfair."

Mara studied her. "We need every suspicion, Miss Linden. Every name is a thread."

Clara took a breath.

"It's Martin Ellsworth. The owner of the Christmas Market."

Hale frowned. "The market organizer?"

"Yes," Clara said. "He's always smiling. Too much. And when people disagree with him, he gets... intense. But quietly. Like there's something underneath."

Mara wrote the name down. "Ellsworth. Possible lead."

Clara's face reddened. "I'm not accusing him. He's kind. He's always helped with charity drives."

Mara tapped the paper. "Cheerfulness can be a mask. Forced optimism can be a coping mechanism—or a weapon."

Hale exhaled slowly. "We'll pay him a visit. For now, we keep following the pattern."

Mara nodded. "Because trust me... the sender is only getting started."

The Christmas Market Interrogation

The Wintervale Christmas Market was a dazzling stretch of holiday stalls wrapped with garlands, twinkling lights, and festive music humming through outdoor speakers. Children ran with gingerbread cookies; couples drank hot cider; tourists admired handcrafted ornaments.

It was cheerful.
Almost too cheerful.

And Martin Ellsworth—its founder and coordinator—stood at the center like a conductor of merry chaos.

He was a man in his late forties with a bright green scarf, rosy cheeks, and a smile so wide it practically sliced his face in half. When he saw Hale, Clara, and Mara approaching, he clapped his hands joyfully.

"Detective Hale! Miss Linden! And—oh—someone new! Welcome to the best place in Wintervale! Isn't it magical today? I swear, the snow fell just perfectly for—"

"Mister Ellsworth," Hale said, cutting through the man's overflowing enthusiasm. "We have a few questions."

"Of course, of course! Always glad to help the law. How can I brighten your day?"

Mara muttered, "He's almost performing."

Hale stepped closer. "Have you seen anything strange around the market recently? Anyone suspicious? Anyone leaving packages?"

Martin's smile faltered for half a second.

Just half a second.
 But Hale noticed.

"Oh well—strange? Hmm. You mean besides strangers coming to admire the stalls? Not particularly! This place is filled with joy, Detective. Suspicious behavior isn't really in the spirit."

"Have you seen this?" Hale asked, holding up the parchment from door three.

Martin blinked at the message.

Then blinked again.

"Oh my. That's... unsettling. Goodness. Is this part of that calendar you received, Clara?"

Clara nodded. "Yes. Today's clue."

"Horrible wording," Martin said, shaking his head vigorously. "Not trusting cheerful people? What a dreadful sentiment."

"Why do you think someone would write it?" Mara asked casually.

Martin smiled again—too quickly. "Oh, you know how some folks can be this time of year. Stressed. Tired. Jealous of others' happiness."

"Jealous of yours, perhaps?" Mara added.

Martin let out a laugh that sounded slightly too sharp. "Me? Oh, heavens no. I'm just a man who loves Christmas! Loves making people happy."

Mara's eyes narrowed.

Hale pressed. "Did you know a man named Rowan Vexley?"

Silence.

For the first time since they arrived, Martin's smile dropped entirely.

"What did you say?"

"Rowan Vexley," Hale repeated. "He made coded wooden calendars. Similar to the one Clara received."

Martin swallowed.

Then forced his smile back into place like gluing a broken ornament together.

"No. Never heard the name. Sorry."

But the tremor in his hands said otherwise.

Clara watched Martin closely. "Is everything alright? You look... shaken."

"Oh! Just cold!" he said, laughing nervously. "Terribly cold today. Must be the wind."

But there was no wind.

And no cold strong enough to cause that kind of tremble.

Mara leaned toward Hale as Martin busied himself handing out candy canes to children.

"He's hiding something."

"Yes," Hale murmured. "But is he the sender... or the next target?"

Clara shivered. "The clue said not to trust the cheerful. And Martin... he's almost aggressively cheerful."

Hale tucked the parchment back into his coat. "Keep your distance from him for now."

As they walked away from the market, Hale turned back.

Martin watched them leave.
His smile gone.
His eyes sharp, calculating, almost... afraid.

Not of them.

But of something else.

Something—or someone—who was watching Wintervale just as closely.

Chapter 4

Silent Nights, Dark Truths

The Fourth Door Opens

December 4th dawned with a fragile quiet, the kind that might have felt peaceful in any other town. But in Wintervale, peace had become a stranger. The morning light was pale and uncertain, filtering through a mist that clung to the hills like a warning left unsaid.

Detective Elias Hale stood in Clara Linden's kitchen, the advent calendar placed carefully on the table between them. Clara had insisted he be there before she opened the next door — yesterday's coded warning still hovered like a shadow neither of them could define.

Mara Keats leaned against the counter, arms crossed, her face unreadable. The coffee she'd poured earlier had gone untouched, steam long vanished.

Clara's hands trembled as she touched the tiny brass hinge of **Door Four**.

"I'm scared to open it," she whispered.

Hale didn't sugarcoat it. "We need to know what the sender planned next."

Clara nodded, swallowing. She eased the little wooden door open.

Something slid out — not parchment this time.

A photograph.
 Small. Grainy. Black and white.

It showed the Christmas Market. Taken at night. Lights blurry, stalls faint in the background. But the focus wasn't on the scenery.

It was on the figure in the center.

Martin Ellsworth.

His broad smile was frozen in the shot, yet something about the picture made it look like a grimace. The photo had been taken from far away, like someone watching him from the shadows.

Clara's voice quivered. "Why Martin again?"

Mara snatched the photo and flipped it over.

A date was written in slanted handwriting.

December 4th — Midnight.

Below it, a second message:

"SECRETS LOOK BRIGHTEST IN THE DARK."

Hale leaned closer. "This isn't a clue. This is an appointment."

"With Martin?" Clara asked, panic rising.

"No," Mara whispered. "With whoever's hunting him."

Hale grabbed his coat. "We're going to find Martin. Now."

The clock read 7:12 a.m.

Whatever was planned for Martin...
 they were already too late.

A Chilling Discovery

The Christmas Market was quiet at this hour, its cheerful glow replaced by a gray stillness. Snow had accumulated overnight, turning the colorful stalls into white-capped huts. A few stall owners arrived early, hauling crates of pastries and garlands, but the usual holiday music was absent. Someone had forgotten to turn on the speakers — or perhaps no one wanted cheerful music today.

Hale, Clara, and Mara crossed the square. Clara shivered; the air felt wrong, heavier somehow.

Martin's primary stall — a bright red-and-green booth decorated with ribbons — stood closed.

"Martin?" Clara called gently. "Are you here?"

No response.

Mara stepped around the side. "Something's off."

Hale noticed it too. Snow around the stall had been disturbed — shallow footprints, partly erased by fresh snowfall. Someone had been here recently.

He tried the latch on the stall door.

Unlocked.

Hale opened it cautiously.

Inside, it was dark. Too dark. He switched on his flashlight.

That was when Clara screamed.

Martin Ellsworth hung suspended from a rafter beam, a thick red-and-white holiday ribbon knotted around his neck like a grotesque Christmas bow. His feet dangled inches above the wooden floor. His usually rosy cheeks were bluish-gray. His eyes were open wide, frozen in terror.

Clara stumbled back. Mara caught her before she hit the ground.

Hale approached the body, jaw tightening. "Cut him down."

Mara untied the ribbon carefully while Hale supported the body's weight. Martin's body slumped heavily into Hale's arms before they laid him gently on the floor.

Clara covered her mouth, tears running freely. "He...
he was just here yesterday. Smiling. Laughing. He
can't—"

"He's gone," Hale said quietly.

Clara sobbed harder.

Mara stood, scanning the area. "This isn't a suicide."

Hale nodded. "No way Martin climbs up and hangs
himself with decorative ribbon. Someone staged this."

She pointed upward. "See that beam? The ribbon is
looped over it at an angle Martin couldn't have reached
alone. And look—there are scuff marks on the stool
near the corner."

Hale examined it. "Someone stood there."

Mara added, "Also look at the knot on the ribbon. This
is a double constrictor knot. Most people can't tie this
cleanly unless they've practiced."

Clara wiped her eyes, trembling. "So... he was
murdered. And the killer put him on display in his own
stall."

"Yes," Hale said.

"In a Christmas ribbon," Mara murmured. "They wanted symbolism. A statement."

Clara looked at the photograph they'd found behind door four. "The calendar gave us the warning. But we didn't get here in time."

Hale closed Martin's dead eyes gently. "We need to search for clues. Anything."

Clara stared down at Martin's limp hand. Something was clasped in it.

"Detective..." she whispered. "There's... something in his fist."

Hale pried it open carefully.

A small piece of paper.

Another parchment fragment.

He unfolded it.

"HE LIED TO YOU ALL."
"LOOK FOR THE LIFE HE NEVER LIVED."
"THE CALENDAR KEEPS SCORE."

Clara shivered violently.

Mara exhaled. "We need answers. Fast."

Suspects Multiply

By midday, Wintervale was buzzing with fearful whispers. Word spread fast — someone running past a stall owner, another sending a frantic message through the Wintervale Neighbors app — within an hour, everyone knew Martin Ellsworth had been found dead.

Hale stood in the town hall, now temporarily converted into an incident room. Maps of Wintervale were pinned on boards. Photographs of the advent calendar clues were laid out on a long table. Martin's photo — alive and staged — sat beside the photo of his body.

Clara sat on a bench nearby, eyes red but focused. Mara stood beside her, holding a notebook and a pen.

Hale addressed them.

"We have to figure out who Martin really was. People with secret lives tend to leave trails. Someone wanted those secrets exposed."

"Who would want him dead?" Clara whispered. "He never hurt anyone."

Mara raised an eyebrow. "Clara, the calendar suggests he did more than hurt someone. It suggests betrayal. Hidden truths."

"Meaning?" Clara asked.

"Meaning," Mara said gently, "Martin may not have been who you thought he was."

Hale stepped forward. "We're looking at three initial angles:

1. Personal secrets
Something in Martin's past — debts, enemies, relationships.

2. Professional deception
The market, the charity funds, any local organizations he was involved with.

3. The calendar connection
Why did the killer warn *him*? Why was he the target of door four?"

Clara hesitated. "I... I know something. Something Martin told me once."

Mara leaned in. "Go on."

Clara bit her lip. "Last year, near Christmas, he told me he hadn't always lived in Wintervale. That he came here because this town felt 'safe.' Like he could start over." She looked from Hale to Mara. "Start over from what?"

Hale sighed. "We'll need to look into his real background."

"Which leads to suspects," Mara said. "And Wintervale suddenly has a lot of them."

She opened her notebook, listing names:

SUSPECT LIST

1. **Gretchen Morrow** – owner of the bakery stall

   - Had arguments with Martin over booth placement

   - Owes money to the market fund

   - Known to hold grudges

2. **Pastor Gregory Tull** – local church leader

- Martin volunteered at church events

- Rumors say Martin once threatened to expose something he learned in confession

- Possible motive: fear or retaliation

3. **Harper Lane** – local journalist

- Investigating Wintervale charities

- Claimed Martin was "too clean to be real"

4. **Darren Loxley** – electrician for the market

- Fired last month by Martin

- Angry, vocal, drinking heavily

Clara frowned. "You really think one of them could do this?"

"Anyone could," Mara said softly. "That's the problem."

Hale shook his head. "No. The killer is meticulous. Intelligent. Symbolic. They used Martin's own cheerfulness against him."

Mara paced slowly. "And there's something else. The phrase in his hand — 'The life he never lived.' What does that mean?"

Clara looked at the parchment again. "Unless... he told us one life. But he lived another."

Mara nodded. "Exactly."

Hale stood. "We'll interview everyone on that list today. But right now, we need to speak to the person who knew Martin the longest."

"Who?" Clara asked.

"His assistant at the market," Hale said. "A woman named Leila Thorn. She's worked with him for six years."

Clara blinked. "Leila? But she adored Martin."

Mara gave a humorless smile. "Adoration and obsession are cousins, Clara."

Hale gathered his coat. "Let's go."

The Victim's Secret Life

Leila Thorn lived in a small, cluttered apartment above the Wintervale Hardware Store. When she opened the door, her eyes were puffy — she had clearly been crying for hours. Her dark hair was unbrushed, and her hands shook as she tried to steady herself.

"Detective Hale," she whispered. "I heard the news. I... I don't believe it. I just can't."

"Leila," Hale said gently, "we're very sorry. But we need your help."

She stepped aside to let them in.

The apartment was a mix of Christmas decorations, paperwork, market brochures, and half-finished craft projects. Above her desk, pinned to a corkboard, were dozens of photographs.

Every one of them included Martin.

Martin at the market.

Martin decorating stalls.

Martin handing out candy canes.

Martin waving.

Martin laughing.

Clara swallowed. "Leila... this is..."

Leila wiped her eyes. "He was my mentor. My friend. My anchor. When I moved to Wintervale, I had nothing. Martin gave me a job. A purpose."

Mara studied the photographs carefully. "Did Martin ever mention trouble? Anyone who might have wanted to hurt him?"

Leila hesitated.

Hale noticed. "Leila, anything you know could help."

She sank into a chair. "Martin wasn't perfect. I knew that. He hid things. But I never thought..." Her voice cracked.

Mara knelt by her. "Start with the truth."

Leila nodded.

"Martin's real name wasn't Martin Ellsworth."

Clara gasped. "What?"

Leila continued, voice barely above a whisper. "His original name was **Matthew Elridge**. He changed it fourteen years ago. He told me he needed a clean slate."

"Why?" Hale pressed.

Leila looked at the floor. "Because he was involved in something terrible."

"What kind of terrible?" Mara asked sharply.

"A woman died," Leila whispered. "In another town. A small town like Wintervale. The police questioned him. Rumors spread. He was never charged with anything... but the whole town turned against him."

"Her name?" Mara asked.

Leila closed her eyes. "I think... Evelyn Vexley."

Hale's blood ran cold.

Mara stood abruptly. "Vexley? As in **Rowan Vexley**?"

"Yes," Leila said. "Martin told me she was Rowan's sister."

Clara stared. "Rowan Vexley — the artisan? The one you said made the original code system?"

Mara nodded slowly.

Hale stepped back, piecing it together. "If the victim was Rowan's sister..."

"And Martin was somehow connected to her death," Mara continued, "then the sender of the advent calendar might be..."

"Rowan," Clara whispered.

"Or someone close to him," Hale said.

Mara shook her head. "No. Rowan Vexley died eight years ago."

Clara blinked. "Then who is doing this?"

Hale turned to Leila. "Leila, did Martin ever mention Evelyn's family? Anyone who blamed him?"

Leila wiped tears again. "Just that her brother never forgave him."

"Rowan," Clara said softly.

"No," Leila whispered. "There was someone else."

"Who?" Hale asked sharply.

Leila looked at the detective with hollow eyes.

"Evelyn had a child. A son. He was twelve when she died. Martin said the boy hated him — blamed him for everything."

Mara exchanged a chilling look with Hale. "A son..."

Leila nodded. "Martin didn't know his name. But he said the boy 'had eyes that burned with grief.' And that he would grow up seeking revenge."

Clara trembled. "You think the killer is that boy? All grown up?"

Mara exhaled. "Revenge can ferment for decades. Especially when grief defines a childhood."

Hale asked, "Do you know what Evelyn's son looks like?"

Leila shook her head. "No. But Martin always said something strange. He said the boy was quiet. Unusually quiet. And that his silence was... unsettling."

Mara froze.

Hale noticed immediately. "What? What is it?"

Mara whispered, "Eight years ago, when Rowan Vexley was found dead, someone else was mentioned in the case file. A silent witness. A boy who never spoke a word."

Clara swallowed. "Where is he now?"

Mara looked at Hale with sudden, terrible clarity.

"In Wintervale," she said. "He's here."

Leila's voice trembled. "The boy had a name. Martin said it once. A first name only. He whispered it like he was afraid to say it too loud."

"What name?" Hale demanded.

Leila breathed out the word.

"Adrian."

Silence fell over the room.

Clara's heart pounded. "Adrian... who?"

Leila shook her head. "I don't know. But Martin said the boy was intelligent. Too intelligent. That he saw patterns in everything. That he could watch people and understand them without ever speaking."

Mara whispered, "A perfect candidate to create a coded advent calendar."

Hale's jaw tightened. "We need to find this Adrian."

Clara felt sick. "But how? Wintervale has dozens of young men."

"No," Mara said. "Not dozens. A handful. And only one who's always alone. Quiet. Observant."

Hale nodded slowly. "I know exactly who you mean."

Clara whispered, "Who?"

Mara turned to her, voice low and grim.

"**Adrian Slate.** The librarian's assistant."

Clara gasped. "But Adrian is harmless! He hardly talks—"

Mara cut her off. "Silent doesn't mean harmless."

Hale grabbed his coat again. "If Adrian is the killer, he's been planning this for years."

"And Door Five," Mara added, "will open tomorrow."

Clara looked at them in horror.

"What happens tomorrow?"

Mara's expression darkened.

"Something far worse than Martin Ellsworth."

Chapter 5

Countdown to Panic

The Town Meeting

Wintervale had always prided itself on being a peaceful place, the kind of town where problems rarely escalated beyond snow-shoveling disputes or the occasional disagreement about Christmas parade routes. But on the morning after Martin Ellsworth's body was discovered, the town square felt like the center of a storm. Word had spread faster than the wind that howled through the pines on Winter Street. Martin wasn't just dead—he'd been murdered.

By mid-morning, every resident with a functioning pair of legs had crammed inside the Town Hall. The building, usually reserved for holiday craft fairs and heritage committee debates, now buzzed with fear, anger, and wild speculation.

Clara arrived with her coat still dusted in snow. The minute she stepped inside, dozens of eyes swiveled toward her. Some were sympathetic. Others suspicious.

A few seemed to glow with a worrisome curiosity, as if they had already begun crafting their own theories about her involvement.

She kept her gaze forward and walked toward the front, where Sheriff Dunn and Detective Hale stood behind a long wooden table. Dunn's face was pale and tight, the strain of the last twenty-four hours worn heavily across his features. Hale, on the other hand, looked like carved stone—immovable, unreadable, but undeniably in control.

"Let's settle down," Sheriff Dunn called out, tapping a microphone. The feedback screeched, drawing an annoyed groan from the crowd. "Please. Please. Everyone—let's take our seats so we can begin."

People reluctantly shuffled into chairs. Clara slid into the front row. Her heart felt heavy, still absorbing the full horror of discovering Martin. And the fourth clue sitting beside his body.

The Advent Calendar was no longer a quirky mystery—it was a countdown to something much darker.

Detective Hale stepped forward.

"As many of you already know," he began, voice steady, "Martin Ellsworth was found dead last night under suspicious circumstances. Evidence strongly suggests this was a homicide."

A collective gasp filled the hall. Someone in the back began crying softly.

"We also believe his death is connected to the series of clues delivered through the Advent Calendar found on Ms. Clara Bennett's porch."

Dozens of necks craned toward Clara.

She straightened her shoulders. Let them stare. She hadn't asked for any of this.

Hale continued, "This is no longer a private matter. Wintervale is facing an active threat. Until we know who is responsible, everyone should assume they could be at risk."

A murmur rippled through the room.

Linda Markham, the bakery owner, stood abruptly. "Are you saying we have a killer running loose in Wintervale?"

"Yes," Hale replied bluntly. "That is exactly what I'm saying."

His honesty rippled through the crowd like a shiver. Wintervale was not prepared for this. They weren't accustomed to murder or danger or coded warnings placed inside decorative calendars.

Dunn took the microphone. "We're organizing curfews, patrols, and safety checks. Starting tonight, nobody—nobody—walks home alone after dark."

The town erupted in chatter.

"My daughter walks from the diner every night—she's not doing that anymore!"

"Is the Christmas Market canceled?"

"What about the tree lighting?"

"Is it true Martin had enemies?"

"Was this connected to the artisan who disappeared years ago? What was his name—Rowan something?"

Hale raised a hand, commanding silence.

"We are asking for full cooperation. Anyone who received unusual messages, anonymous packages, or has seen someone lurking around their property—report it immediately. Even if it seems small."

Clara stood. Her voice felt shaky at first, but strengthened as she spoke.

"Whoever left that Advent Calendar wanted me involved. They're playing a game—and using this town as the board."

All eyes fixed on her again.

She continued, "Martin didn't die because of something random. He was chosen. And until we figure out why, none of us are safe."

A heavy silence settled across the hall.

Finally, Beatrice Crowley—Wintervale's self-appointed historian—rose with trembling hands.

"Detective Hale," she said, "I don't mean to alarm anyone further... but our town has seen this before."

A hush fell.

Hale leaned forward slightly. "Explain."

Beatrice swallowed. "Twenty-five years ago. Before many of you lived here. A similar string of events took place. Cryptic messages. A coded ledger. A missing person. The case was never officially solved."

Clara felt her pulse stop.

Detective Hale's expression revealed only one thing: interest.

"Whose case?" he asked quietly.

Beatrice looked down, then back up.

"Rowan Vexley," she whispered.

The room erupted once again.

Clara felt the ground shift beneath her feet.

The Advent Calendar wasn't a game.

It was a legacy.

A message from the past resurfacing—with vengeance.

A Break in the Case

After the meeting finally adjourned, Hale motioned for Clara to follow him into a side office. The space was small and cluttered, filled with dusty filing cabinets and holiday decorations that someone had never gotten around to storing properly. A plastic wreath leaned against a stack of boxes marked **TOWN RECORDS – DO NOT REMOVE**.

Hale shut the door behind them.

"That woman—Beatrice Crowley," he said. "Has she ever mentioned Rowan Vexley to you before?"

Clara shook her head. "No. I barely know her."

Hale paced once, twice. "Rowan Vexley disappeared twenty-five years ago. No body ever recovered. His family left town shortly after. Case went cold—fast."

"And you think it's connected to what's happening now?" Clara asked.

He stopped pacing.

"I think someone wants us to believe it is."

He dropped a folder onto the table between them.

Inside were the four clues found so far. Clara felt a chill just looking at them.

Door 1 — **Don't trust the cheerful.**
Door 2 — **What was buried never stayed dead.**
Door 3 — **Patterns reveal what people conceal.**
Door 4 — **The past always collects its debts.**

She forced herself to breathe. "Are you saying Rowan Vexley might be alive?"

"I don't rule anything out," Hale said. "But if he is... he's had twenty-five years to plan something."

Clara stared at the clues. "Martin was cheerful. Too cheerful. Whoever wrote the clues predicted his death."

"Or orchestrated it," Hale said quietly.

Clara gulped.

"Detective," she said, "I've been thinking... these clues aren't random. There's structure. Intent. What if the killer isn't just sending warnings? What if they're narrating their next move?"

Hale's jaw tightened.

"That's exactly what I'm afraid of."

He reached into the folder again and pulled out a slip of paper.

"This arrived at the station this morning."

He handed it to Clara.

Her breath caught.

It was another clue—but not from a door.

This one was on thick paper, neatly folded, with the same looping handwriting.

You're already behind.
Day Five waits for no one.

Clara's heart slammed against her ribs.

"What does that mean?" she whispered.

Hale's expression darkened.

"It means the calendar is going to strike again today."

The Calendar Strikes Again

The snow fell in thick curtains as the afternoon deepened into a blue-gray haze. Wintervale looked beautiful, almost serene—utterly deceptive considering what was brewing beneath the surface.

Clara walked beside Hale toward Winter Street, where the houses lined up like gingerbread sculptures dusted in white. Despite Hale's insistence that someone accompany her everywhere, Clara felt exposed, as though unseen eyes tracked her from every rooftop and frosty window.

Her porch came into view.

Clara gasped.

A new package sat waiting for her.

Not the small decorative doors she had received before. This one was larger—maybe the size of a shoebox—and wrapped in shimmering gold paper with a deep red bow. It looked festive, even luxurious.

It also radiated menace.

Hale walked ahead of her, one hand on his holster. He approached the box like it was a live explosive.

"It's too big for one door," Clara whispered.

"That's what scares me," Hale replied.

He crouched beside it, studying the edges carefully. "No tripwire. No mechanism visible."

Clara swallowed. "Is it safe to open?"

Hale didn't look convinced, but he nodded. "Stand back."

Clara stepped behind him as he lifted the lid.

Inside was a small velvet pouch, deep crimson. Hale opened it slowly.

A note slid out first. Thick cardstock. Inked in the same looping script that haunted Clara's dreams.

Door Five:
Truth shatters.
Secrets splinter.
Listen closely, Clara.
You won't have long.

Clara's blood ran cold.

Hale reached deeper and pulled out something metallic.

A recorder.

An old-fashioned silver voice recorder, scratched along the sides but still functional.

Clara's breath caught. "Why would the killer send us that?"

Only one reason made sense.

Hale pressed play.

Static crackled.

Then a voice—not the killer's—burst through the speaker.

"...someone's following me... I don't know who... It can't be happening again..."

Clara froze.

She recognized the voice.

"Martin," she whispered. "That's Martin."

The recording continued. Martin sounded breathless, panicked.

"...if anyone finds this... it wasn't an accident... I was warned... said I had to keep quiet about—"

A loud crash echoed in the recording.

Martin's scream followed.

Then silence.

Clara staggered back against the railing, gripping it tightly.

"He knew," she whispered. "He knew he was going to die."

Hale replayed the last line slowly.

"Said I had to keep quiet about—"

"It cuts off," Clara said breathlessly. "We never hear what he was keeping quiet."

Hale turned the recorder over in his hand. "This is deliberate. The killer wants us to know Martin had a secret."

Clara looked toward the street.

The world suddenly felt smaller, darker.

"And they want us to know he wasn't the only target."

The wind howled through the trees, carrying a whisper of dread through Wintervale.

Betrayal Under the Lights

That evening, the entire town gathered again—this time outside in the Christmas Market square, where the lights cast a warm glow over the frightened faces of Wintervale's residents. The atmosphere was tense, as if the holiday decorations themselves were holding their breath.

Sheriff Dunn addressed the crowd, but his voice lacked the authority it had that morning. Too much had happened. Too much had been revealed.

"We'll be increasing patrols around Winter Street," he said, sounding tired. "No one should be walking alone—"

He didn't get to finish.

A shout erupted from the left side of the square.

Clara and Hale whipped their heads toward the noise.

Linda Markham, the baker, was pushing through the crowd, her face red with fury.

"You," she hissed, pointing directly at Clara. "You need to tell them what you saw!"

Clara blinked. "What I saw?"

Linda stormed closer. "You think the rest of us haven't noticed? Every clue delivered to you. You always right there when something happens. You're not innocent in this!"

Murmurs of agreement spread.

Hale stepped forward sharply. "That's enough."

But Linda wasn't backing down.

"Maybe she knows more than she's saying," Linda snapped. "Maybe Martin wasn't the first one she—"

Clara's shock turned to anger. "How dare you. I found Martin. I called for help. That's it."

"Then explain this!" Linda pulled something from her coat pocket and thrust it toward Hale.

A piece of red cardstock.

With Clara's name on it.

Clara felt her knees weaken.

The card was identical to the Advent Calendar notes.

Hale snatched it, turning it over.

Another clue.

**Traitors hide in plain sight.
The one you trust most will betray you.**

Hale's eyes flicked to Clara.

Clara's heartbeat crashed into her ribs.

"I didn't do this," she said, voice barely audible. "Detective, I swear. Someone planted that on her."

Linda scoffed. "Oh please—"

But before she could continue, the Christmas Market lights flickered once, twice—

Then went completely dark.

Gasps and screams filled the air.

Clara reached out blindly. "Hale?"

A hand grabbed her wrist.

But it wasn't Hale's.

A voice whispered close to her ear—too close.

"Day Six is coming, Clara.
 And it's your turn."

Clara screamed.

The lights snapped back on.

People rushed around in panic.

But whoever held her...

Was gone.

Hale fought his way to her side. "Clara! What happened?"

Clara's voice trembled.

"He was here," she whispered. "The killer. He touched me. He spoke to me."

Hale grabbed her shoulders. "Did you see him? Hear anything else?"

Clara shook her head violently. "No. Just that. Just that one message."

Hale's jaw tightened.

"We're running out of time," he said. "The killer is escalating."

Clara looked around at the crowd—at faces twisted with fear, suspicion, and confusion.

The killer had been right there among them.

Watching.

Taunting.

Choosing the next door to open.

And Clara knew one thing with absolute certainty:

Wintervale's nightmare had only just begun.

Chapter 6

The Final Twelve

A Race Against Time

The morning of December 6th arrived with the brittle clarity of a Wintervale winter dawn. The snow that had carpeted the town for the past several days now gleamed like a frozen ocean under the weak sun, the rooftops shimmering in silver and gold. But the town's beauty was a cruel contrast to the chaos that had gripped its residents since Martin Ellsworth's murder. Fear had become a constant companion.

Clara Linden woke to the sound of sleet tapping against her bedroom window. Her mind churned through the events of the last few days: the advent calendar's sinister clues, Martin's death, the mysterious recording, and the whispered warnings of a killer hidden in plain sight. Each event pressed down on her like a weight she could not shake. And now, Day Six had arrived.

She dressed quickly, pulling a thick wool coat over her nightclothes. Her heart pounded as she approached the front door, her breath forming clouds in the cold morning air. The Advent Calendar sat on her table as it always did, a silent herald of terror. She had been warned: the final twelve doors were coming, and with them, the stakes would rise to a level she was not sure she could survive.

Detective Elias Hale arrived shortly after she stepped outside. His presence was a comfort, though his expression carried the same rigid tension it always had since the nightmare began. Mara Keats followed behind, notebook in hand, scanning the town as they walked. Clara noted that the normally bustling streets were strangely quiet. Even the early morning shoppers seemed to sense that something malevolent had taken root in Wintervale.

"We're behind," Hale said quietly, breaking the silence. "The killer is moving faster than we anticipated. We can't afford delays."

Clara nodded. "I know. But where do we even start today? Every clue has been a trap, every step forward seems to bring more danger."

Hale's eyes narrowed. "We start by thinking like them. The Final Twelve aren't just random. They're a countdown. Each door is a puzzle, each step a test. Whoever is doing this knows how to manipulate fear—and they're counting on us to panic."

The three of them approached Clara's porch. On the doorstep, there was a small envelope, sealed with deep crimson wax. Clara's hands shook as she picked it up. She broke the seal carefully, revealing a sheet of thick paper inscribed in the familiar looping script.

"Time is a candle burning fast.
 Six remain. Move wisely, or the final flame will consume all."

Clara shivered. The words were chilling, but they also contained a cruel taunt. The killer's mind was a maze, and they were daring her to navigate it correctly. Failure was not an option. Hale stepped forward, scanning the surroundings as he spoke.

"Whoever wrote this is precise. They know we're watching. They're testing our reactions, measuring our panic. Today, the traps will tighten. Be ready."

The trio moved swiftly toward the town center. Every footstep through the snow felt like a countdown itself, each crunch underfoot echoing the tension in Clara's chest. As they passed the Christmas Market, she noted that the area was eerily deserted, save for a few cautious merchants who peered out from behind the barricades. Even the festive lights that usually danced along the stalls seemed muted, casting shadows that felt unnatural, almost predatory.

"Clara," Mara said, breaking the tense silence, "we need to track patterns. The first four doors were leading us toward someone, somewhere—but each one also revealed secrets about Wintervale. If the killer's logic holds, Door Six will bring the final truth closer, but it will also be the most dangerous."

Clara swallowed hard. "And if we're wrong?"

Hale's jaw tightened. "Then Wintervale may not survive this."

A Clue Hidden in Carol Lyrics

The next clue was delivered in an unexpected way. Unlike the previous envelopes and photographs, this one arrived in the form of a small cassette tape tucked beneath the branch of a pine tree near the town's central square. Mara spotted it first, carefully pointing it out before anyone else could approach.

"Tape?" Clara asked, raising an eyebrow. "Who even uses tapes anymore?"

"Someone old-school," Hale said, frowning. "Or someone who wants this to feel deliberate, tactile. There's a reason they didn't just send another note."

Clara's hands trembled as she picked up the tape. The label was handwritten in the same cursive, crimson-inked script she had come to recognize. It simply read: **"Day Six — Listen Carefully."**

Hale produced a small tape player he had retrieved from the evidence room at the station. Mara perched beside Clara, notebook ready.

The tape clicked as Hale pressed play.

Static hissed.

Then, faintly at first, a voice began to sing. Soft, lilting, almost like a carol:

"Silent night, holy night...
All is calm, all is bright...
Round yon virgin mother and child..."

At first, Clara thought it was harmless—familiar. But as she listened, her stomach tightened. Interwoven with the lyrics were subtle anomalies: a pause here, a word stretched unnaturally there, and then, faintly, a whisper beneath the melody:

"...behind the wreath... under the pine... six lies hidden..."

Clara's eyes widened. "It's a code. The lyrics are pointing to something in the market."

Hale nodded. "Exactly. The killer uses every detail in the town to craft their clues. A carol is no longer just a song—it's a map."

Mara flipped through her notebook. "We need to break this down line by line, and watch for anomalies in rhythm, syllables, pauses. The voice may even be manipulated to emphasize locations or numbers."

They retraced the song carefully, repeating it aloud. Clara felt her pulse quicken as a realization struck her.

"The reference to a wreath and a pine..." she whispered. "There's a large evergreen near the center of the square. And the main wreath is above the mayor's office. That has to be it."

Hale's eyes flicked toward the tree. "Then that's where we start. Carefully."

The Wintervale Archives

The evergreen proved a critical point. Beneath its snow-laden branches, partially hidden by the lower limbs, Mara discovered a small metal box. It was locked, but its surface bore an intricate engraving that matched the style of the Advent Calendar's final doors: an interwoven pattern of holly, stars, and tiny numeric symbols.

Clara crouched beside Mara. "Another puzzle," she murmured. "Of course it is."

Hale knelt, inspecting the lock. "Nothing here is random. Whoever designed this calendar knew the town intimately—knew where people would look, and how we'd respond."

Mara produced her tools, carefully picking the lock with delicate precision. The box clicked open, revealing a series of folded papers and a key.

Clara picked up the first sheet. The paper was yellowed and brittle, unlike the crisp notes from the calendar. Its handwriting was jagged, hurried, and undeniably older.

The note read:

"To those who seek truth:
 Wintervale keeps secrets in shadows.
 Look where the town's memory sleeps.
 The Final Twelve begins where stories are kept."

Clara frowned. "Memory... stories... Wintervale archives?"

Hale's eyes narrowed. "Exactly. This is our next stop. Whoever the killer is, they're pointing us toward the town's history. There's a pattern here—they're forcing us to confront the past in order to prevent the future."

They hurried to the archives, a small brick building tucked between the post office and the town library. Its windows were frosted, its doors locked, but Hale produced a master key. Inside, the archives smelled of dust, old paper, and varnish. Rows of metal filing cabinets stretched toward the ceiling, each drawer labeled with years and subjects.

Clara scanned the cabinets. Mara started sorting through ledgers with meticulous care, while Hale examined old news clippings and town records. The three worked in tense silence, acutely aware that each minute might bring the next move from the killer.

After nearly an hour, Clara unearthed a ledger that made her blood run cold. Its cover was embossed with the Wintervale crest and the words: **"Town Council, 1985–1995."** Flipping through, she discovered a series of entries marked with small red symbols—almost invisible unless the pages were held just so. They chronicled deaths, disappearances, and mysterious accidents, many of which had been attributed to misfortune or misadventure. But one name recurred: **Rowan Vexley.**

Clara felt a chill. The past and present were colliding in ways she hadn't anticipated. The killer was drawing them closer, step by step, and the town itself was the puzzle board.

The Killer's Shadow

As the afternoon faded into evening, the trio emerged from the archives with more questions than answers. The snow had turned slushy underfoot, and the glow of the Christmas lights gave Wintervale an otherworldly, almost sinister beauty.

Clara's hands trembled as she held the key from the metal box. It was old, cold, and heavy, as if it carried the weight of the secrets it unlocked. The pages from the archives rattled in Mara's hands.

"We're getting close," Mara said. "The pattern of the calendar... the messages... it's leading us somewhere. But the closer we get, the more dangerous it becomes."

Hale glanced around the square. The shadows from the lampposts stretched unnaturally long across the snow, bending toward them like dark fingers. "The killer is watching," he said softly. "They've been with us all day, in plain sight. Every shadow, every flicker in the light—look closely. That's where the killer lives."

Clara shivered. "Every day... I feel like we're one step behind. Like they're laughing at us."

"You're not wrong," Mara said. "The calendar is more than a set of clues—it's psychological warfare. They want us paranoid, divided, and desperate."

Suddenly, a subtle sound drew their attention—a footstep on slush behind a distant storefront. Hale's hand went instinctively to his holster. Clara's heart raced. Mara's notebook clutched tightly in both hands.

They turned slowly, but no one was there. Only the empty street, the lampposts, and the whispering wind. Yet all three of them felt it: the shadow of someone present, unseen, calculating.

Clara whispered, "They're always close."

"Yes," Hale said grimly. "And the Final Twelve will not forgive mistakes."

As they retreated toward the safety of the patrol car, Clara realized something terrifying: the killer was no longer content to target Martin or leave cryptic notes. They were weaving Wintervale itself into a trap, using the town's history, its geography, and its people as pieces on a deadly chessboard. Every step, every action, every decision—was being anticipated.

Clara glanced back at the archives, at the glowing streets of Wintervale, and at the snow-dusted rooftops.

The killer's shadow was everywhere.

And tomorrow, with Door Seven, it would strike again.

Chapter 7

Christmas Eve Confession

The Twenty-Fourth Door

The night of December 24th descended upon Wintervale like a velvet curtain, the stars above pale and distant in the cold winter sky. The streets were silent except for the crunch of snow underfoot, each step echoing like a ticking clock counting down the final hours of a nightmare that had gripped the town for weeks.

Clara Linden walked alongside Detective Elias Hale and Mara Keats, her breath rising in white plumes that mingled with the fog of the streetlights. Each of them carried a small lantern, the warm glow doing little to dispel the icy dread that had settled in their bones. The advent calendar sat in Clara's satchel, its wooden structure heavy with anticipation. The final door—the twenty-fourth—was waiting, its brass hinge gleaming like a jewel in the lantern light.

"We're finally here," Clara whispered, more to herself than anyone else. "Twenty-four days... twenty-four doors... and now the last one."

Hale's expression was unreadable, as always, but Clara could see the tension in his shoulders. "Final doors are the deadliest," he said quietly. "The killer's mind is behind this. Each step we've taken, each clue we've followed... it's all led here. Be ready for anything."

Mara, notebook in hand, nodded. "We know the pattern. We've followed their game. But this... this is different. The final door isn't just a message. It's a confession, or a trap, or both. And we cannot underestimate it."

Clara's hands trembled as she reached for the final door. The brass was cold against her fingers. She took a deep breath and lifted it.

Inside was a single envelope. The handwriting was jagged and urgent, more aggressive than any previous note. Clara tore it open and unfolded the paper. Her eyes skimmed the words, and her stomach sank:

"You've followed the path. You've uncovered the lies.

**The truth is closer than you think.
Meet me at the center of Wintervale at midnight.
Everything ends there."**

Clara's pulse raced. Midnight was less than an hour
away. The center of Wintervale—the town square
where the Christmas Market had once been—was
precisely where Martin had been found. And now, it
was where the final act would unfold.

A Truth Too Terrible to Ignore

The trio hurried toward the town square. Every lamp
post cast long shadows that seemed to twist and writhe
in the snow, shapes forming like fingers reaching for
them. The weight of the last twenty-four days pressed
upon Clara, and for the first time, she allowed herself
to imagine the true horror that awaited.

"This is it," Hale said, voice low. "The killer knows
we're coming. Everything is prepared. Every detail is
orchestrated. Stay sharp."

Clara's mind raced. **What truth could be so terrible
that it required twenty-four days of psychological
torment?** She had seen the body of Martin Ellsworth,
heard his final warning on the tape, followed the clues

hidden in carols, and sifted through the Wintervale archives. Every revelation had been worse than the last, and now the final truth waited.

Mara spoke softly. "Whatever we find tonight, it will change how Wintervale sees itself—and how you see everything you thought you knew."

Clara clenched her fists. "I'm ready. I have to be."

They arrived at the square just before midnight. Snow fell lightly, muffling sound and casting a surreal glow over the familiar yet haunted landscape. The Christmas lights flickered, as if struggling to stay bright against the gathering darkness. In the center of the square, someone waited. Their figure was wrapped in a dark coat, hood drawn, face hidden.

Clara's stomach churned. This was it—the confrontation.

The figure stepped forward, slowly, deliberately. The voice that followed was muffled at first, then clear, ringing across the snow-covered square.

"Clara Linden. Detective Hale. Mara Keats. You've come exactly as I expected."

Hale's hand moved toward his holster, but Clara stopped him. "Wait. Let's hear them out first."

The figure pulled back their hood slightly, enough to reveal a glimmer of identity—but not enough to fully recognize them. The voice continued:

"You've followed my games, uncovered my traps, and survived the past twenty-four days. But now you will understand why it had to happen this way."

Clara swallowed hard. "Why Martin? Why the others? Why all of this?"

The figure's tone was almost sorrowful. "Martin was the beginning. He wasn't innocent, though he seemed so. The calendar was never about punishment alone—it was about revelation. About truth. About exposing the lies that Wintervale has hidden for decades."

Clara's heart pounded. She remembered Martin's confession in fragments—the secrets he had kept, the child of Evelyn Vexley, the shadow of Rowan Vexley's disappearance. And now the killer's voice confirmed her worst fears: **the town's sins were being laid bare.**

The figure extended a hand, revealing a small bundle wrapped in gold paper. Clara's breath caught. "What is that?"

"Your final clue," the figure said. "Inside is everything you need to understand."

Clara approached cautiously, untied the ribbon, and opened the package. Inside was a folder filled with documents, photographs, and letters—evidence connecting every thread of the past twenty-four days.

Clara began reading. Her eyes widened as she realized the scope of the deception. **Martin had been hiding debts, alliances, and betrayals. The Wintervale council had covered up incidents from decades ago. Families had been wronged. Lives had been manipulated. The killer was not just one person—they were the culmination of vengeance and justice, meticulously planned.**

Mara stepped closer. "This... this is more than a confession. It's a map of the town's hidden truths."

Clara shivered. "And the killer... they know I'll see it all. They're counting on me to understand it."

The Final Confrontation

The square seemed to contract around them. Snowflakes fell like frozen knives, cutting through the quiet. Clara looked at Hale. "Do we stop them now? Or wait?"

Hale's eyes were intense. "We wait. We listen. Any move too soon, and the truth may be lost—or worse, someone else may die."

The figure spoke again, voice echoing. "Everything you've endured was necessary. Martin, the calendar, the messages, the terror... it was all to prepare you for this. To prepare Wintervale for what must be known."

Clara's mind raced. She realized the killer's plan wasn't simply to punish—they wanted recognition, acknowledgment of the sins buried beneath Wintervale's picturesque surface.

"Enough words!" Hale finally broke in. "Step forward and face the consequences. The terror ends tonight."

The figure laughed softly, a sound that carried both sadness and menace. "Consequences? You misunderstand. The consequences have been ongoing, in every moment you've walked through this town.

Every shadow, every secret, every lie—it has been part of the reckoning. I am not the cause of fear. Fear has always been here."

Clara's hands shook. "Then what do we do? How do we end it?"

The figure slowly revealed themselves further—enough that the lantern light fell across a familiar face, yet still partially obscured. They reached into a pocket and pulled out a final envelope, identical to all the others.

"This is Door Twenty-Four," the figure said. "Inside, the truth you cannot ignore. You will finally see why Wintervale's shadows have always been waiting for this night."

Clara's pulse surged as she took the envelope and opened it. Inside was a letter, typed and signed only with a symbol—a snowflake etched with a single slash through its center.

Her eyes raced over the words:

"Clara,
 You have followed the path. You have seen the consequences of hidden lives, of unspoken grievances.

Tonight, Wintervale changes. Not because of me, but because of all that has been concealed for too long.

Do not seek to forgive. Do not seek to punish. Understand. Only understanding allows the town to survive.

The final twelve were never about endings. They were about awakening."

Clara staggered backward, absorbing the weight of the message. Hale placed a steadying hand on her shoulder.

"Awakening," she whispered. "All of this... it wasn't just terror. It was... teaching us."

Mara shook her head. "Or testing us. The killer remains out there. The shadow remains. They've forced every secret into the light, but they've not yet revealed themselves. That's the danger—the reckoning is still incomplete."

The figure, now fully obscured in the darkness again, spoke one final time:

"Wintervale will never be the same. Remember the calendar. Remember the doors. And remember: not all truths bring peace."

Then they vanished into the night, leaving only the snow and the flickering lanterns.

A Town Forever Changed

As the first snowflakes of Christmas Eve drifted across the square, Clara, Hale, and Mara surveyed the scene. Residents had gathered, drawn by the commotion, their faces a mixture of relief, confusion, and lingering fear. The town had survived the calendar's horrors—at least for now—but everyone understood that Wintervale itself had changed.

Families huddled together, whispering about the revelations contained in the documents Clara held. Shopkeepers discussed the secrets revealed about the council. The history of Martin, Rowan, and the hidden grievances of decades past rippled through conversations like an undercurrent of frost, binding the community in shared shock.

Clara felt exhausted, her body trembling from the day's events. "Will it ever stop?" she asked, voice barely above a whisper. "The fear, the secrets, the shadows?"

Hale placed a hand on her shoulder. "No. But Wintervale has been forced to confront what it has always avoided. That's survival. That's understanding. And perhaps... in that, there's hope."

Mara looked around the square. "The killer's shadow may linger, but we've forced the light into every corner they could hide in. Wintervale will remember tonight—not for terror alone, but for the truths finally unveiled."

Clara glanced at the Advent Calendar, now empty, its final door open and its final message delivered. The wooden structure felt strangely light in her hands, as if the burden it carried had been partially lifted.

She thought of Martin Ellsworth, of Adrian Slate, of the unnamed victims of the past, and of the town itself—forever altered by the Final Twelve. And she realized that Wintervale would never return to the simplicity it had once known.

But perhaps that was the point. Perhaps the calendar, the clues, the terror, had been a reckoning long overdue.

As the clock struck midnight, Clara looked up at the star-filled sky and whispered, "Merry Christmas,

Wintervale. May we survive what we've learned—and may we never forget it."

Hale and Mara stood beside her, silent, understanding that the night marked both an end and a beginning. The calendar's terror had concluded, but the consequences of the truths revealed would ripple through the town for generations.

And in the shadows, the killer's presence lingered still, unseen but unmistakable, a reminder that not all games are finished—even when the final door has been opened.

Chapter 8

After the Frost Settles

Healing in Wintervale

The first rays of sunlight pierced the crisp morning sky over Wintervale, glinting off rooftops and icicles alike, as though the town itself were slowly waking from a long, harsh dream. Snow still blanketed the streets, the frost glinting like shards of crystal, but there was a quiet beneath the winter white, a fragile calm that contrasted sharply with the chaos of the previous days.

For Clara Linden, the quiet was both a relief and a burden. The calendar had ended, the Final Twelve doors had been opened, and yet the weight of everything she had witnessed refused to lift. She walked slowly through the town square, where residents were tentatively emerging, shovels in hand, sweeping paths through the snow. Conversations were hushed, cautious, as if everyone feared stirring a shadow that might still be lurking.

Shops reopened, albeit cautiously. Windows displayed festive decorations that had seemed bright and cheerful before the calendar's dark influence had begun—but now even tinsel and lights seemed touched by uncertainty. Families gathered in small clusters, exchanging quiet words of concern, whispering about secrets uncovered, and memories of Martin, Rowan, and the missing pieces of Wintervale's past.

Clara approached the town library, its doors open to the public once more. The archives, which had been the center of so much tension just days ago, were now calm and orderly. She watched as people hesitated before entering, curiosity battling with lingering fear.

Detective Elias Hale was already there, quietly overseeing the reorganization of the historical records. He noticed Clara and motioned for her to join him.

"Wintervale is waking up," he said softly. "People are cautious, yes. But they're also beginning to confront what has been buried. That's the first step toward healing."

Clara nodded, though her stomach was heavy. "It feels strange," she said. "The terror is over, but everything we discovered... the lies, the betrayals, the deaths... it's like the town has been scorched. Can Wintervale truly recover?"

Hale's gaze was steady. "Recovery isn't about forgetting. It's about acknowledgment. About ensuring that the shadows that controlled the past don't dominate the future. The calendar forced us all to see the truth, and now Wintervale has the chance to rebuild—not in denial, but with understanding."

Mara Keats joined them, holding her notebook tightly. "Some of the townspeople are already beginning to talk about reforms," she said. "How to prevent corruption, how to honor those who were overlooked. It's a start."

Clara took a deep breath. She felt the snow crunch beneath her boots and thought about Martin Ellsworth, Adrian Slate, the hidden lives revealed through the calendar, and the ghost of Rowan Vexley that had hovered over the town for decades. Wintervale had survived the terror, but it would never again be the same.

And perhaps, she thought, that was a blessing.

The Case That Haunted Christmas

Though the immediate threat had passed, the shadow of the calendar lingered like a faint frost across every corner of Wintervale. Newspapers chronicled the events in meticulous detail: Martin Ellsworth's death, the twisted puzzles of the Advent Calendar, and the revelations unearthed from the archives. Headlines screamed of "A Christmas Horror in Wintervale" and "Secrets Buried in Snow," capturing the attention of not just local readers but those across the state.

Inside the police station, Hale and Clara reviewed the case one final time. The physical evidence—the notes, the envelopes, the tapes—was now cataloged and stored, but the psychological impact was far from resolved.

"Every Christmas from now on," Hale said, leaning back in his chair, "someone in this town will remember the calendar. Every holiday cheer will carry the memory of fear. That's the legacy of what we faced."

Clara nodded slowly, flipping through her notes. "And yet... it also brought the truth to light. Martin's secrets, the town council's misdeeds, the hidden stories of

Rowan Vexley... people finally know what was happening behind closed doors."

Hale's expression softened, though his eyes remained vigilant. "Yes. The case haunted Wintervale, and it haunted us. But understanding is the only antidote to lingering fear. That, and vigilance. The calendar might be finished, but there are always lessons to be learned."

Mara, who had been quietly observing, added, "It also reminded us how fragile trust can be, how quickly secrets can fester. Wintervale's people will need time to rebuild that trust—not just with each other, but within themselves. And that's a healing process that will take years."

Clara looked out the window at the snow-dusted square below. Children were beginning to play cautiously in the fresh snow, parents standing nearby, keeping watchful eyes. Life had returned, fragile but persistent.

"And what about the killer?" Clara asked quietly. "We still don't know who orchestrated all of this. They vanished before the final confrontation. What happens if they strike again?"

Hale's jaw tightened. "Then we hope the lessons we've learned and the vigilance we've developed will be enough. But for now... we watch, we prepare, and we remember."

Redemption and Reflection

The days following Christmas were marked by introspection and subtle rebuilding. Wintervale's residents began to reconcile with the town's hidden past, holding meetings, restoring old archives, and supporting one another. Families who had been estranged over years of small grievances found themselves reconciling in the shadow of the larger horrors they had all witnessed.

Clara, despite the lingering trauma, found a new sense of purpose. She dedicated herself to cataloging the notes and documents, ensuring that the story of Wintervale's ordeal would be preserved—not as sensationalized gossip, but as a warning and a testament to the power of truth.

Mara Keats published a careful account of the events, emphasizing the psychological impact of the calendar and the importance of confronting hidden histories. Her work earned attention far beyond Wintervale, drawing experts in behavioral analysis and criminal psychology to study the case.

Hale continued his work in law enforcement, quietly ensuring that the town remained safe. Though the killer's identity was still unknown, his presence in Wintervale—his vigilance, his strategy, his insight—remained a stabilizing force.

One evening, Clara walked along the quiet streets with Hale and Mara. The town was illuminated by the soft glow of holiday lights, casting long shadows that seemed almost peaceful now. She reflected on the lessons of the past twenty-four days: courage, persistence, and the necessity of facing uncomfortable truths.

"Do you ever think about the people who came before us?" Clara asked, her voice low. "The ones whose secrets led to this... the ones we'll never meet?"

Hale nodded slowly. "All the time. That's the weight we carry. But it also gives us the chance to make things right moving forward. Redemption isn't just about fixing mistakes—it's about learning from them, and teaching others to do the same."

Mara added, "And reflecting on what fear can teach us. It's a terrible teacher, but sometimes it brings clarity. The calendar forced the town to confront its shadows. Now, the choice is ours: do we let fear dominate, or do we let it guide us toward vigilance and truth?"

Clara's gaze fell on the now-empty Advent Calendar sitting on her mantle. It seemed so small, so innocuous—but she knew the power it had held. The terror it had unleashed, the secrets it had revealed, and the lessons it had forced upon Wintervale were indelible.

And yet... in its aftermath, there was hope. Even in a town forever changed, even in a town marked by shadow and sorrow, there was a possibility for renewal.

One Last Unopened Envelope

As the first week of January settled over Wintervale, the town began to regain a sense of normalcy. Snow continued to coat the streets and rooftops, but the shadows had lifted, leaving clarity in their place. Life had resumed, and yet there was an unshakable feeling that something remained unresolved.

Clara entered her home late one evening, exhausted but determined to continue her work documenting the events. She approached the mantle where the Advent Calendar had been displayed. There, beneath the dust and soft glow of candlelight, she noticed something she hadn't seen before: a small, slender envelope, tucked carefully behind the calendar.

Her heart skipped a beat. She had assumed every door had been opened, every clue examined. And yet, this envelope had eluded her, hidden in the shadow of the final door.

With trembling hands, she pulled it free. The envelope was unmarked—no crimson wax, no looping script, nothing to indicate its origin. It felt almost... alive in her hands.

Clara hesitated. "Should I open it?" she whispered to herself, the air in the room suddenly thick with tension.

Hale's voice echoed in her mind: *Vigilance. Lessons. Understanding.*

Summoning her courage, she carefully broke the seal. Inside was a single card. Clara unfolded it slowly, her eyes scanning the words:

"Not all endings are final. Not all truths are complete. Remember the lessons of Wintervale, and never forget the shadows that dwell where secrets are kept. The game is over... but the consequences will always remain."

Clara's hands shook. She felt a shiver run down her spine—not from fear, but from the realization that the story, the calendar, and the shadow that had haunted the town were not fully extinguished. The killer remained unseen, their presence hinted at even in absence.

Hale and Mara entered quietly, sensing her tension. Clara held up the card.

"It's the last envelope," she said. "We never saw it before. And now... it feels like a warning. A reminder. That the calendar's influence, the lessons it taught, may never truly leave Wintervale."

Mara's eyes widened. "It's a parting message... or perhaps a challenge. The killer may be gone, but their shadow remains."

Hale nodded, placing a reassuring hand on Clara's shoulder. "And that's a reminder to us all. To never take the calm for granted, to never ignore the secrets beneath the surface, and to remain vigilant—because even after the frost settles, Wintervale's history will always echo in the snow."

Clara folded the card carefully and placed it in her notebook. For the first time in weeks, she felt a sense of quiet resolve. The town had endured, and she had survived. But she also knew that Wintervale would never be the same—and that the calendar's lesson, the shadow it left behind, would be remembered for generations to come.

As the snow fell softly outside, Clara, Hale, and Mara sat together in the warm glow of the hearth. They had survived the terror, uncovered the truth, and witnessed the shadows that lurked beneath the town's surface. Wintervale was scarred, yes—but it was also awake.

And in the silence of that snowy night, one truth became clear: even in darkness, understanding can bring light—and even the longest winters eventually yield to spring.

Acknowledgements

Writing *The Advent Calendar Murder* has been a journey marked by long nights, quiet mornings, and the constant hum of imagination weaving itself into the town of Wintervale. Though this story is a work of fiction, it was shaped, strengthened, and guided by many people whose encouragement and presence turned an idea into a full-fledged novel. I am deeply grateful to each of them.

First and foremost, I want to thank everyone who has supported my writing from the very beginning. Whether you offered a word of confidence, a late-night conversation, or a reminder to keep pushing forward, you played a part in the creation of this book. Writing can often feel like a solitary endeavor, but the support of thoughtful, patient, and kind people makes all the difference. You reminded me that stories are not just written—they are shared, embraced, and carried by others.

To my friends who listened to my endless plot twists, theories, and revisions: thank you for never once pretending to be tired of hearing about Wintervale's secrets. Your enthusiasm fueled mine, and your feedback helped me refine the twists, deepen the suspense, and stay true to the heart of the story. Every time you asked, "What happens next?" you pushed me to write the next chapter.

To the readers—whether this is your first book of mine or you've followed my writing journey before—thank you for choosing to step into this world. Mystery readers are among the most observant and thoughtful, always searching for patterns and details hiding in the shadows. I wrote this book with you in mind, hoping to give you a story filled with tension, warmth, fear, hope, and all the emotions that swirl around the holiday season. Your time is valuable, and I am honored that you spent it with this story.

A special thank you goes to those who keep the spirit of reading alive: independent bookstore owners, librarians, reviewers, bloggers, and the countless individuals who champion stories of all kinds. In a world overflowing with noise, you make room for books to be discovered. You are the quiet heroes who connect stories to the hearts meant to read them.

To my creative inspirations—both the old mysteries I grew up with and the modern thrillers that continue to raise the standard—I owe gratitude for teaching me the craft, the rhythm, and the delicate balance between tension and emotion. The tradition of mystery writing is long and rich, and I am honored to contribute my own small piece to it.

Lastly, thank you to everyone who believes in the magic of storytelling. Wintervale may be fictional, but the courage, fear, love, and resilience found here are reflections of truths we all experience. This book would not exist without the shared human desire to explore the unknown, confront hidden darkness, and ultimately find light again.

From my heart to yours—thank you.